HONEY'S
Dance Recital

by
ALEXANDRIA CUNNINGHAM
Illustrations by MIKE MOTZ

*To my mother, Debra Carson,
God's industrious bee.
Writing began with you and
will now continue on with me.
Thank you for working hard
and encouraging a legacy
that will change our family
for generations to come.
Cheers to Honey!*

ACKNOWLEDGMENT:

To the most stellar dance girls I know:
Caroline Collins, Lane Edmonds, Brandi
Edwards and Haleigh Triplett. -A.C.

HONEY'S
Dance Recital

by
ALEXANDRIA CUNNINGHAM
Illustrations by MIKE MOTZ

Honey was sweet like the morning dew. She lived in a yellow house with her mom, dad, twin brothers, and stuffed panda, Bangles. She was silly, quirky, and loved helping others. Honey was good at many things, especially dance.

"It's finally here! It's finally here! Listen big brothers, the time is near," Honey said as she sashayed to the table. "Good morning, Honey! We see someone's excited about their recital today," Honey's brothers said.

Honey couldn't wait to dive into her meal. She enjoyed breakfast with her family. It was the one time of day they would eat together because of their busy schedules. Each morning, Honey ate cheese in her eggs and butter in her grits.

With no time to waste, Honey said her goodbyes.
"See you later, alligator, rotten tomato, hot potato."
Honey ran to the door where her mother was standing,
waiting to take her to rehearsal.

"I'm sure Miss Lynnberry is waiting Honey. Let's get
to it." Honey's mother hurried her along.

Honey loved the dance academy so much and couldn't wait to see everybody dancing. When her mother arrived, she opened the door, grabbed her bag, and twirled inside.

"Good morning, girls! Today you get to show off all your hard work. We'll practice the show, have lunch, then go backstage for hair and make-up," Miss Lynnberry said with cheer.

Marlee took the lead for warm up. "Feet together, grab your wrist, and begin happy feet."

"Grab your left wrist with your right hand. That is what I recommend," said Honey.

"I know which hand, Honey." Marlee glared.

"Whelp, I was just trying to help," said Honey.

The girls went on practicing their routine, moving their feet to first position, then second and fourth.

"You're supposed to cross your legs, you scrambled egg," Honey said.

"I know-www!" said China.

"Whelp, I was just trying to help," said Honey.

On to the ballet bar, the girls practiced plies.
"Bend your knees, Demi," said Honey.
"I know how to plie, Honey," said Demi.
"Whelp, I was just trying to help," said Honey.

The girls were tired, and it was time for lunch.
"Hey, China, want some of my fruit punch?" Honey
asked.

"Not from you, Honey Boo," said China.

"Hey, Marlee, I saved you a seat. I hope you like
luncheon meat," Honey said.

"Sorry, Charlie. I'm having pizza," said Marlee.

"Hey, Demi, do you want to sit by me?"
Honey asked.

"Sorry, Honey. Obviously my knees
don't bend enough for me to sit," Demi
said.

Sadly, Honey finished her lunch alone, then trudged
backstage for hair and make-up. She held back tears as
she pulled Bangles out of her bag and gave him a hug.

"I don't know why my friends are being so mean. It's not like I'm being a cruel recess queen," Honey whispered.
The girls finished their lunches and were all dolled up for the recital.

"Places, ladies. Places," Miss Lynnberry whispered. The house was full, and the curtains would be opened soon.

"Honey, stand in second," whispered China.
"No, Honey, you should be in fifth," said Demi.
"She should definitely be in third," proclaimed Marlee."
"There is no third!" China and Demi declared.

The curtains rose, and the music began to play. Confused on where to begin, Honey made up a routine right on the spot. Tendu front, Tendu back. Demi plie, full plie, and THUMP!

Honey fell onto the floor. Embarrassed, she stood up and ran backstage. The dancers gasped and ran behind her.

"Honey, are you alright?" her mother asked.
"Sure, I'm alright. I gave myself a fright," Honey said. "I forgot my routine then my legs turned into noodle cuisine."

With Demi and Marlee standing by her side, China said, "It's our fault. We confused Honey on purpose. We knew it was wrong, but we wanted to get back at her for correcting everything we did during practice."

"Girls, thank you for your honesty, but that was very mean," said Honey's mother. "What should you all say?"

"We're sorry, Honey."

"I apologize banana pies," said Honey. "I should have focused on my own part instead of correcting you sweet tarts."

"Thank you all for those warm apologies," Miss Lynnberry said. "Now let's give these people the show that they've been waiting for."

At the end of the show, Honey received a bouquet of yellow roses.

"Besides the fall, you did great overall," Honey's brothers laughed.

"Job well done, Honey bun," said Honey's dad.

"Thanks, everyone. It was fun. Can you get me a snack? I'll be right back," Honey asked.

Honey gave each of her friends a yellow rose. "Look, they match our bows," said China.

"They mean friendship, honey dips," said Honey.

"Thanks, Honey." The girls giggled as they hugged.

ABOUT THE AUTHOR

Alexandria "Allie" Cunningham grew up in Northport, Alabama. As a child, she wrote short stories and acquired many notebooks of daily journal entries. Writing is, and has always been, one of her passions. Allie is an early childhood and elementary school teacher. She lives in Alabama with her husband, Kirstan, and their dog, Kemper Kai.

Made in United States
Orlando, FL
24 May 2022